Merry Christmas 2003!

Love,
Mrs. Thompson

SECRETS *of* THE VINE™ *for Kids*

By Dr. Bruce Wilkinson
Adapted by Melody Carlson
Illustrated by Dan Brawner

Thomas Nelson, Inc.
Nashville

SECRETS OF THE VINE™ FOR KIDS

Published in Nashville, Tennessee, by Tommy Nelson®,
a Division of Thomas Nelson, Inc.

ISBN 1-4003-0053-3
LC Control Number: 2002067095
LC Classification: BV4501.3 .Wt

Printed in the United States of America

02 03 04 05 WRZ 6 5 4 3 2 1

Contents

INTRODUCTION iv

CHAPTER ONE

Get Closer 1

CHAPTER TWO

What Does It Mean? 15

CHAPTER THREE

When We Blow It 27

CHAPTER FOUR

Love Can Get Tough 41

CHAPTER FIVE

Shear Madness? 53

CHAPTER SIX

"Grape" Expectations! 67

CHAPTER SEVEN

Hang On! 77

CHAPTER EIGHT

The *Best* Friend 89

CHAPTER NINE

Humongous Harvest! 97

INTRODUCTION

God created YOU for a purpose: He wants you to have a TOTALLY fantastic life!

HE CREATED YOU in this special way so you can enjoy a relationship with Him. And, as a result, He can do miraculous things through you. He wants you to have a life filled with purpose and mission and real excitement!

Listen now to some of the **last words** Jesus spoke. See if you can begin to understand their ***secret*** **meaning.**

> *I am the true vine, and My Father is the vinedresser. Every branch in Me that does not bear fruit He takes away; and every branch*

that bears fruit He prunes, that it may bear more fruit. . . . ***I am the vine,*** *you are the branches. He who abides in Me, and I in him, bears much fruit; for* ***without Me you can do nothing****. . . . By this My Father is glorified, that you bear much fruit; so you will be My disciples. As the Father loved Me, I also have loved you; abide in My love. . . . You did not choose Me, but* ***I chose you and appointed you*** *that you should go and bear fruit, and that your fruit should remain. . . .* (John 15:1–2, 5, 8–9, 16*a*)

I want this book to help **bridge the gap** between you and Jesus Christ—between today and two thousand years ago. Through it, you will **understand the mission He left you** (and all of His followers) during His last night on earth.

I invite you to come to the vineyard with me now. Draw close to Jesus and **hear His final lesson.** It is one of the most powerful lessons of all time. Experience for yourself the *Secrets of the Vine.*

Chapter One
Get Closer

Everyone wants a *best* friend. You want a special person you can laugh or cry with, someone you can trust with your deepest secrets. You want a loyal friend who will be there for you in the good times and the bad. But sometimes friends let us down. Maybe your friend moved away or decided he wanted to hang out with someone else. Or maybe she's never home when you call. Then what?

He really likes you, too!

You probably feel let down, lonely, maybe even hurt. But did you know you have a friend who will *never* do any of those things? This friend will always be there to listen, to care, to hang with you when you feel lonely. And He will

This friend has given His everything to be there for you— not just when it's convenient, but every minute of every day— 24/7.

always laugh with you when you're glad. This friend has given His everything to be there for you—not just when it's convenient, but every minute of every day—24/7.

You may have guessed this friend's name: Jesus Christ. And maybe you already know that Jesus loves you. But guess what? He doesn't just love you. *He really likes you, too!* And the coolest part is that He wants to be your *very* best friend. He wants you to know how much He has in store for you. He wants you to see how great your life can become when you ask Him to be your very best friend. So, right now, come along with Him. Share in the very last moments of His life on earth. And hear His final words to discover God's amazing plan for you.

THE LAST NIGHT

What if your very best friend were about to move away? What if you had only a few hours left to spend together? How valuable would that time be? Now imagine that your friend had something really important to say to you.

"Listen carefully," he might say.

Would you pay better attention then?

"I have to tell you something," he might add. "I waited until now . . . but I can't wait any longer."

I know that Jesus wants His meaning to be perfectly clear.

Would you cling to his words, hoping to remember them forever?

Now what if that person about to speak were Jesus? How closely would you listen to Him?

This little book is about Jesus' last message. It's about what He said to His disciples on the night He was arrested and taken away. Within twenty-four hours, Jesus would be nailed to the cross. A day later He would die.

So Jesus knew His final words were important. And He hoped His last lesson would echo in His friends' ears for years. He hoped His words would change His friends' lives, and even their way of thinking, forever!

But Jesus' last teaching is often misunderstood by today's believers. Most of us aren't very familiar with vineyards or with how grapes grow. This teaching might seem mysterious, like a secret even. And that's why I call this lesson *Secrets of the Vine.*

I know that Jesus wants His meaning to be perfectly clear. I know He wants all of us to understand exactly what He taught that night. Only then can we be ready for the great life God has in store for us. It doesn't matter how old (or young) we are. God has a plan that will start to unfold when we listen to Him and begin to understand this mystery.

So come with me now, and experience how our Savior shared His unforgettable secret.

They **knew** Messiah **would deliver them** **and all of Israel,** from their enemies—forever!

A FINAL MEAL

You've heard about the "Last Supper." Maybe you've even seen a painting that shows Jesus

and His disciples gathered around a table filled with food. In a way, it was like a Thanksgiving feast, except the men sat on the floor, leaning on pillows.

It was a time of celebration—the night before the big Jewish celebration of Passover. And Jesus' friends probably felt pretty good when the evening started. They already knew that their friend Jesus was Messiah (the Promised One sent by God). And they knew Messiah would deliver them, and all of Israel, from their enemies—forever! What a time to celebrate! Or so they thought.

Why was their Messiah doing a servant's job?

WHAT'S GOING ON?

When supper ended, Jesus stood up. He took off His robe. Then He poured water into a big bowl and knelt down to wash His disciples' feet!

His friends watched, surprised. What was

Jesus doing? They felt uncomfortable as their leader scrubbed between their dirty toes. It was embarrassing, too! But no one dared to speak. Still, they wondered: *Why was their Messiah doing a servant's job?*

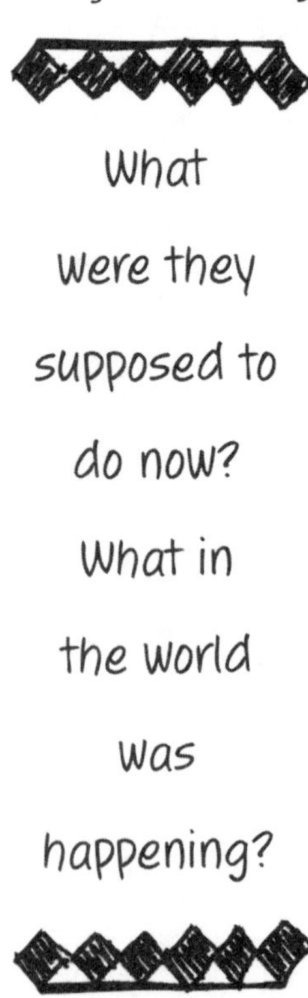

Next, Jesus surprised them again by saying that one of His good friends would betray Him. Stunned by this news, the men looked around the room. Who would do that? And then Jesus told Peter that before the next day, Peter would say that he never knew Jesus, not just once but *three times!* That evening, Jesus' disciples felt their whole world turn upside down.

Of course, Jesus had tried to make His mission clear, right from the beginning. The problem was, the disciples just hadn't been listening. They'd

Jesus chose His words carefully. He wanted to make a point—a point they would never forget!

wanted an earthly king, someone who had power and glory. They had heard only what they'd wanted to hear.

But that night Jesus warned them, "A little while longer and the world will see Me no more." His friends grew sad. *Where is He going?* they wondered.

Jesus continued. "I will no longer talk much with you, for the ruler of this world is coming." Now His disciples became even more confused. Did this mean Jesus would *never* be king? They thought the whole purpose of Messiah's coming was to rule the world. But it sounded like Jesus planned to leave. What did this mean?

Jesus had called them His "little children," but they were full-grown men. And He said, "I have loved you . . . ," and "Let not your heart be troubled. . . ." What was Jesus really hinting at? The more they wondered, the less His disciples must have understood. They must have just stared at Jesus in stunned silence. Finally, He said, "Arise, let us go from here."

Can you imagine the confusion as they followed their leader into the night?

Perhaps they carried lamps or torches, but their journey was probably pretty dark and silent. And how did the disciples feel as they walked through Jerusalem? Did they feel worried or frightened? After all, they'd given up everything to follow this man.

What were they supposed to do now? What in the world was happening?

THE VINEYARD STORY BEGINS

The disciples followed Jesus from the noisy city streets into the Kidron Valley. Perhaps Jesus stopped in a vineyard that night, a quiet place where He could get His disciples' full attention. Surrounded by rows of grapevines, Jesus

Can I talk you, heart to heart, for a moment? If you've never really given your life to Jesus, then *stop*. Ask yourself: *Am I ready to receive Jesus into my heart?* If not, what are you waiting for? He promises that if we ask Him in, He'll come. It's really that simple. If you decide to invite Him into your heart, you'll meet the best friend you'll ever make. And you'll begin to live the life God has in store for you!

paused. His disciples might have watched with curiosity. They probably wondered why He was reaching for a grape branch.

"I am the true vine," He began, *"and My Father is the vinedresser"* (John 15:1).

His disciples probably listened politely as Jesus told them all about branches and grapes and how to care for a vineyard. But they might not have understood. Jesus chose His words carefully. He wanted to make a point—a point they would never forget!

THE SECRET

Obviously, you and I didn't hear the words Jesus spoke to His disciples that night. But did you know that He meant His message for you, too?

Even now, Jesus has lovingly drawn you to this book, just like He drew His closest friends into a vineyard so long ago. He wants to share His secrets with you—so you can experience even more of His wonderful plan for your life. So let's look carefully at His words and see what secrets they hold.

FRUIT
BRANCH
VINE
VINEDRESSER

Chapter Two

What Does It Mean?

et's list some of the things that Jesus did *not* talk about in the vineyard.

Talk about grapes.

He didn't mention money.

He didn't say anything about wearing a crown or sitting on a throne.

He didn't pull out a map or military plan. (Some of His followers had hoped He would take over Jerusalem by force.)

No, Jesus wanted to talk about grapes. But why grapes?

Jesus often taught by using word pictures. In His stories, He helped people see (in their minds) something familiar. Then He explained how to look at that thing in a new way. In this case, Jesus talked about a

This vine is more like a trunk. It grows out of the ground and supports the rest of the plant.

vineyard because everyone understood about grapes back then.

Jesus wanted His disciples to see how important it is to stay connected. Maybe if He taught this lesson today, He'd use the Internet as His example. But in Jesus' day, people knew as much about vineyards as you do about computers. He could illustrate this same kind of connection by pointing out the parts of a vineyard.

Let's look closely at each part.

THE VINE

Jesus said, *"I am the true vine"* (John 15:1).

Okay, you might think of a vine as the long, skinny, winding part of a plant that climbs up your grandma's fence in the summertime. Not so with a grapevine. With grapes, the vine is more like a trunk. It grows out of the ground and supports the rest of the plant. A healthy vine has a root system that goes deep into the soil to draw water into the plant. This water gives the plant life. It becomes sap, which flows through the vine and into the branches. Eventually, it produces juicy grapes. A well-kept vine grows about three or four feet tall. And it's sturdy enough to feed a whole system of branches. The vinedresser usually supplies some sort of support for these branches.

THE VINEDRESSER

Jesus said, *"My Father is the vinedresser"* (John 15:1).

The vinedresser's task is simple: to take care of the plants and help them produce as many

The vinedresser's task is simple: to take care of the plants and help them produce as many grapes as possible.

grapes as possible. The better the vinedresser cares for a vineyard, the more grapes it will produce for harvesting at the end of the season.

THE BRANCHES

Jesus said, *"You are the branches"* (15:5).

Lots of branches can grow out of each grapevine. Each branch usually grows in a different direction, and each one bears fruit. The branches get fed by the vine, which helps them to grow and climb. And the vinedresser ties these sturdy branches to supports so they don't get too heavy and break. The healthier and stronger the branch, the more grapes it will grow.

Each branch usually grows in a different direction, and each one bears fruit.

THE FRUIT

Jesus said, *"You should go and bear fruit"* (15:16).

The goal behind all the hard work of tending, pruning, weeding, and watering the grapevines is to get a whole lot of grapes to harvest. In other words—it's all about the fruit. And with the right care, each branch can grow lots of grapes.

AND THE POINT IS?

Okay, so Jesus is the vine, God is the vinedresser, and we're the branches, right? But what lesson was Jesus trying to teach?

First, Jesus wanted to paint a vivid picture in our minds. We can keep that picture with us our entire lives to remind us of our purpose. And Jesus knew that we needed an easy-to-remember illustration. By saying that He is the vine and we are branches, He showed us just how much we need Him. How can a branch possibly survive without a vine? And He reveals how important it is to stay connected to Him: We draw our life directly from Him. Finally, He shows us God's role.

Bearing fruit for Jesus will bring us more joy than anything else in the world.

God cares for us as the faithful vinedresser: He watches over us and supports us.

But the really exciting part of this story is that, as branches, we can bear fruit! And bearing fruit for Jesus will bring us more joy than anything else in the world.

Just what does it mean to bear fruit? Keep reading and I'll show you.

FOUR BRANCHES AND FOUR BASKETS

Imagine you're in a vineyard right now, just walking along in the sunshine. Maybe you

pluck a grape or two. Maybe you decide to see if you can juggle a few grapes.

Up ahead you notice a really big vine with four thick branches. The branches shoot out in four different directions. You know the vine-dresser has just finished picking the grapes from each branch.

You walk up to the vine and peek into the baskets sitting beside it. You expect to see all four baskets brimming with grapes. But you discover that each basket has a very different number of grapes inside.

To your surprise, the first basket has no grapes at all. You look carefully at the branch above the basket and see that it doesn't look too healthy. Some of the leaves have wilted, and a part of the branch has fallen down into the dirt.

To your surprise, the first basket has no grapes at all.

You check out the next basket. It looks a little better. You can see several clusters of grapes in the bottom, but those wimpy grapes don't look very appetizing. Why didn't the second branch grow more grapes?

But when you look into the third basket, you start to smile. This basket definitely has more fruit than the first two combined! And the fruit looks full and sweet. Even though the basket's not completely full, you wouldn't mind taking this one home.

Then you glance over at the fourth basket. Wow! This basket takes the prize! It has so many big, luscious, purple grapes that it can't hold them all. They tumble over the sides. And they smell even better than homemade grape jam! How amazing that a single branch could produce so much fruit!

How amazing that a single branch could produce so much fruit!

Jesus used the example of these four different branches to describe the sorts of lives we can live. We can be like those wimpy and fruitless branches or like the ones that are healthy and covered with grapes—or anywhere in between. But our ability always depends on how well we stay connected with our vine (Jesus) and how we respond to the care of our vinedresser (God).

In other words, the fruit in your own basket is all about *relationship*.

Basket #1: "No Fruit" (15:2)
Basket #2: "Fruit" (15:2)
Basket #3: "More Fruit" (15:2)
Basket #4: "Much Fruit" (15:5)

WHICH BASKET IS UNDER YOUR BRANCH?

So, if you believe in Jesus, you are one of His branches. But did you know that you already have some grapes in your basket? Jesus knows exactly how many because He sees what's going on in your life—every single day. He knows when we do something good for Him.

So, if Jesus checked your branch today, how many grapes would He find to harvest? Which basket do you think best describes your life? Which basket would you like it to be? Which basket do you think God wants for you?

> *By this My Father is glorified, that you bear* **much fruit.** (John 15:8)

God wants us to follow Jesus with our whole heart. And He wants us to have completely full—even overflowing—baskets. He knows that's what will make us really happy, too. Can you imagine how you'd feel if at harvest time you had only a shriveled clump of grapes? And how would you feel when you saw fat, juicy grapes spilling out of other baskets? Can you see that God wants you to have that heaped-over kind of joy when you present your harvest to Him? He wants us all to share in celebration when we offer full baskets that honor Him. Keep reading to see how you can make sure to fill your basket to overflowing.

You get to choose how much fruit you produce by choosing to live God's way.

Each time we decide to share, or to be polite, or to tell someone about God, another big, juicy grape pops into the basket.

Jesus says, "Each branch bears fruit." You get to choose how much fruit you produce by choosing to live God's way. Maybe that means you'll clean up your room today without needing a reminder. Or maybe you'll help your little sister with her homework. Perhaps you'll take the time to read the Bible and pray. Or maybe you'll make friends with the new kid at school. But whatever it is, you try your best to live your life for God.

test
Today

Chapter Three
When We Blow It

Ling knows how it feels to blow it. She gave her heart to Jesus when she was only seven. And she tried hard to live the way she believed Jesus wanted her to live. In fact, Ling's family and friends saw her as an example of a good Christian kid. Ling also did well in school and started as goalie on her soccer team. But suddenly everything changed.

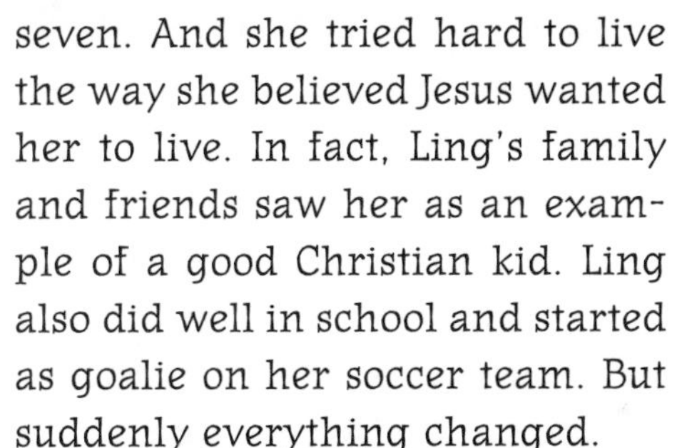

Ling was in fifth grade when her soccer team made it into the play-offs. Excited by thoughts of victory, she spent every spare moment practicing, blocking goals with Ashley (the best goal kicker on the team). But Ling spent very little time doing her

What Ling didn't know would affect her relationship with Jesus.

homework or studying for Friday's big science test. By Thursday, she knew she was in trouble.

"I'm gonna flunk that science test tomorrow," she told Ashley as they left practice.

Ashley laughed and bounced the ball off her foot. "Not me. I've got that one in the hole."

Then Ashley explained that she had the test answers. She offered to share them with Ling—if Ling promised not to tell. Ling knew cheating was wrong, but she also knew her parents would be upset if she failed the test. They might even keep her from playing in the soccer play-offs. So Ling decided to cheat. She told herself that she'd only do it this one time. And she'd make up for it later by studying harder than ever.

But what Ling didn't know was how her decision would affect her relationship with Jesus. Because Ling felt guilty about cheating (even though she aced the test), it suddenly became impossible to pray. Until then, she had enjoyed praying to God about everything. Now she felt guilty all day on Friday. And the next day, when the play-offs started, Ling didn't have fun playing soccer. Then her team lost in the very first game! Ling had let too many goals get past her. She felt totally miserable.

On Sunday, Ling didn't even want to go to church with her parents. She told them she felt sick. In a way, it was true because her stomach did hurt. But she knew it hurt because she was living a lie.

Later in the day, Ling's dad came into her room. "I know something's wrong," he said in an understanding voice. "I want you to tell me all about it."

"It looks like God is trying to teach you something really important."

"The first thing I'll do is ask God to forgive me."

Ling felt so ashamed that she didn't want to tell her dad. Then she realized keeping her secret made her feel terrible. She told him the whole, embarrassing story. Certain her dad would be upset, Ling looked down at the rug and waited.

Finally, her dad cleared his throat. Placing a hand on Ling's shoulder, he said, "It looks like God is trying to teach you something really important."

Ling looked up. "You aren't mad?"

Dad shook his head. "I'm disappointed, but I'm glad you told the truth."

"I really blew it," Ling said miserably.

Dad nodded. "Yes, you did. And I think God is letting you feel so bad because He loves you. He wants you to learn something from this mistake. That's how God disciplines us."

"But what do I do now?" asked Ling.

"I think you already know." Her dad smiled.

"And if you don't, I'm sure that God will tell you, if you ask Him. Then go to your teacher."

Ling sighed. "I guess you're right. I think the first thing I'll do is ask God to forgive me."

During the next week, Ling got her problem sorted out. First, she had a long talk with God. Then she confessed to her science teacher about cheating and received the failing grade she'd earned. Ling didn't tell anyone about Ashley's role, but she did tell her friend that cheating was wrong. Ling even apologized to her teammates for being distracted on the field.

A branch that falls off its support can stop bearing grapes.

A HELPING HAND

When Jesus told His disciples the story about grapevines, He said that branches that didn't bear fruit would be taken away (John 15:2). A more exact translation of the original Greek word (*airo*) is "to lift up."

In a vineyard, branches can slip off their supports and fall onto the ground. Wind blows, dust settles, and the leaves overhead block the sunlight. If it rains, the branch just lies in the mud, where it can get diseased. The problem is, a branch that falls off its support can stop bearing grapes.

Now you might think the vinedresser would come along and just snip those worthless branches right off. They're only good for the compost pile, right?

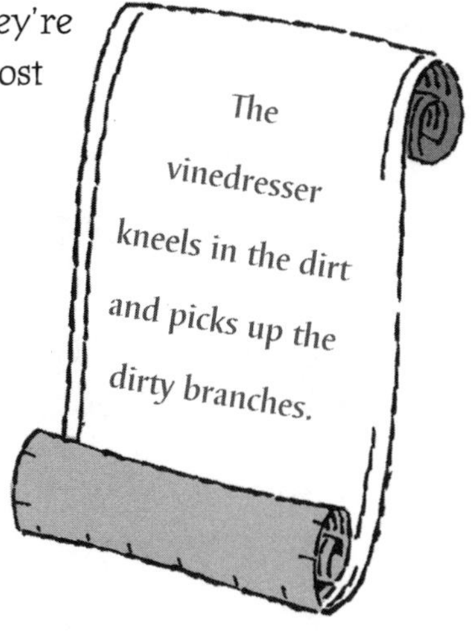

No way! The vinedresser understands that every branch is valuable. And with the right care, even fallen branches can start to make grapes again.

So the vinedresser kneels in the dirt and picks up the dirty branches. He gently washes their muddy leaves. Then he carefully ties them back onto their supports. In time, they grow strong and repay the vinedresser with big, juicy clumps of grapes.

In a way, that's what God was doing with Ling. She had fallen into the mud when she decided to cheat. But God came along and cleaned her off by convicting her of her sin. Then He helped her up and showed her what to do in order to, once again, live her life for Him. God does the same for you and me. He loves us, and He wants what's best for our lives. This brings us to the first secret of the vine.

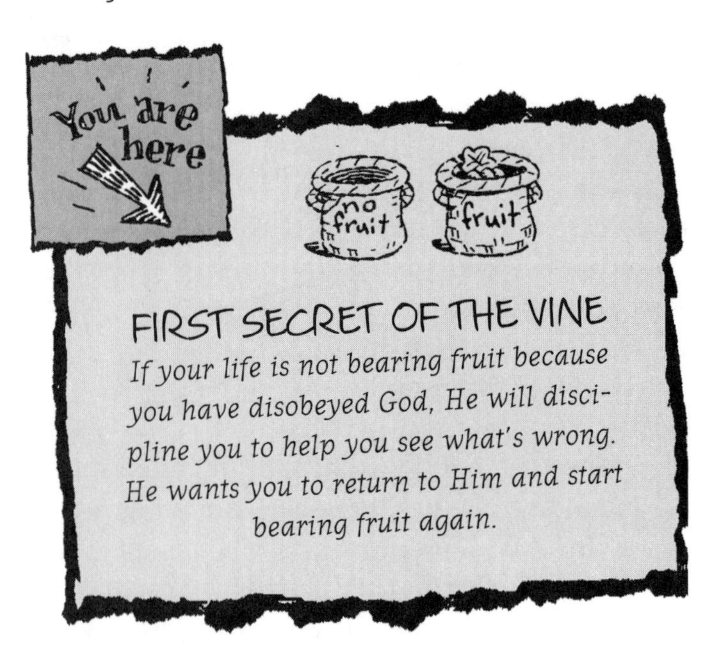

FIRST SECRET OF THE VINE

If your life is not bearing fruit because you have disobeyed God, He will discipline you to help you see what's wrong. He wants you to return to Him and start bearing fruit again.

GROUNDED BY GOD?

Ling knew she was lucky that her dad didn't punish her. But what she didn't realize was that God had disciplined her all along. Remember how guilty she felt?

Even if we don't get in trouble for an action, or if we sin in a way that others can't see, God is always watching. And He disciplines us in the way we feel. Remember how Ling eventually felt so miserable that she couldn't even concentrate on soccer?

If we lie and feel bad about it, that bad feeling is God's discipline. If we steal something but find we can't enjoy using the stolen item, that is God's discipline. We can be sure that God is disciplining us when we stop enjoying our sins.

Sin always leads to regret, guilt, and feeling awful inside. These feelings come to us because the Lord wants us to stop sinning. And through His discipline, God shows us how much He loves us.

Sin ALWAYS leads to regret, guilt, and feeling awful inside.

Bible Snapshot

A Whale of a Bellyache

JONAH KNEW GOD and served Him faithfully. That is, until the day God asked Jonah to do something he didn't *want* to do. God told Jonah to go preach to Nineveh (a nation that had been Israel's enemy). Jonah not only refused, but he also hopped a boat heading in the opposite direction. Jonah tried to hide from God.

So God stirred up a big storm. The crew felt certain their boat would soon sink. They threw everything they could overboard, hoping to keep

their boat afloat. Then they went to Jonah and pleaded with him to pray to God to save them. Jonah knew God was unhappy with him, and he confessed to the sailors that he had run away from God. That's when the crew got really scared.

By then, Jonah knew he was in pretty big trouble. "Pick me up and throw me overboard," Jonah told them. "Then the storm will stop."

And before long, just when it seemed the ship was doomed, the crew threw Jonah into the sea. Instantly, the storm stopped.

Now you'd think Jonah would have drowned in those raging waves. But God had other plans. He sent a huge fish to swallow Jonah whole. And that's just where God kept him for three long days. You can bet that got Jonah's attention. Jonah wept and prayed and eventually apologized to God. And finally, God told the bellyaching fish to go spit Jonah out on a sandy beach.

Jonah knew that God meant business, and he decided it was time to obey. So with seaweed hanging from his hair, he started the long trek to Nineveh. There he finally preached God's message. And to his astonishment, the people actually listened and turned their hearts to God!

IT'S ALL UP TO YOU

Ling and Jonah both made wrong choices. The tough consequences that followed were the result of God's discipline. But how they chose to react to this discipline was entirely up to them. They both had a choice to make: either confess their sins and learn their lessons, or keep suffering the consequences.

How we decide to react to His discipline is entirely up to us.

The same can happen in our lives. We may blow it sometimes. We may purposefully choose to sin—whether we cheat, lie, disobey, steal, gossip, feel envious, or participate in any other sinful behavior. And when we do, God *will* discipline us.

God can use anything, from our own feelings to parents to teachers, to show us the consequences of our bad choices. But how we decide to *react* to His discipline is entirely up to us.

If we resist God's correction, we'll have to live with the shame and grief and mud on our face. But if, like the vine, we accept the loving hand that plucks us from the dirt, then we'll learn from our sin and grow stronger.

God disciplines us so we can live the life He has planned for us. But it's up to us to make good choices. And even though something sinful might *seem* like more fun, we need to remember that Satan loves to trick us. We find true happiness only when we live life God's way. And that makes us able to bear fruit!

CHAPTER FOUR

Love Can Get Tough

What is it with a mom's eyebrow, anyway? When I was a kid, my mom could snap me to attention, jerk my hand from the cookie jar, or make me stop talking mid-sentence—all by raising one eyebrow. "The look" was louder than any words!

I grew up in a family with six kids. If one of us acted up at dinner, Mom's raised eyebrow hinted at immediate trouble. That look meant, *What do you think you're doing?*

The truth is, Mom's raised eyebrow carried weight because I knew from experience what would happen if I didn't pay attention. Mom used her eyebrow to get my attention, to warn me. If

I ignored this warning, and she had to raise her voice to get my attention, then I would probably get grounded or sent to my room. And if I continued to misbehave, I would probably get a spanking from my dad. Now some parents don't spank, but every family has its own discipline stages—usually light, medium, and serious.

GOD'S OBEDIENCE SCHOOL

What are the stages of God's discipline? What methods does He use on you? God has many ways of redirecting His children. And God definitely knows how to get our attention. Like my mom with her raised eyebrow, He starts out with small hints. He hopes we'll get smart and figure things out before He has to raise His voice. Take a moment and check out the three levels of correction God uses to discipline His children:

Level One—Light Correction (like a whisper)

God's first level of discipline (like my mom's raised eyebrow) is a quiet one. He uses a still, small voice to whisper inside you that you're about to do something wrong. And because God loves you, He wants to spare you from the pain this mistake will cause. His whispered warning can be that sort of nervous feeling

This is God shouting. He wants you to stop, right NOW!

that comes over you. Or perhaps you'll feel your heart start to pound, or your palms begin to sweat. Sure, it's only a quiet, gentle nudge. But somehow you know—*you just know*, deep down in your gut—that what you're considering is wrong. *That* is God's whisper of warning. And He wants you to listen and obey.

Level Two—Medium Correction (like a shout)

So you ignored the whispered warning and went ahead and sinned. You disobeyed God. His next form of discipline won't be so quiet. God will have to shout to get your attention now. But since He loves you, He'll keep making the effort to get your attention.

You might notice things start to change and seem beyond your control. You feel unhappy inside, your relationships with family and friends suffer, you have difficulty praying.

Maybe stuff will start to go wrong at school. Just like Ling and Jonah, you may feel like your whole world has begun to cave in on you. This is God shouting. He wants you to stop, right now! He wants you to admit that you've blown it and return to Him. He wants you to tell Him you're sorry and that you're ready to obey.

Level Three—Serious Correction (this might hurt)

Because God loves you, He may allow life's consequences to knock you around a little—and this can get painful. When we don't listen to His whisper and don't pay attention even when things get worse, God has to do something more to get through to us. The fact is, when we keep choosing to disobey, we *will* suffer consequences. We might lose the trust of our family and friends. We might feel shamed by our actions. It's

When we keep choosing to disobey, we will suffer consequences.

possible our reputation will suffer. Sometimes, God permits some pretty painful things to come our way when we refuse to listen to Him.

A PRICE WE PAY TO DISOBEY

The worst consequence is that we hurt our relationship with God. You see, we can't stay close to God while we disobey Him. And you can be sure that if God doesn't immediately get you out of your mess, it's because He wants to get your full attention. He knows that when we feel miserable, we remember to wise up and return to Him. If we ask Him to forgive us, He will!

THE MOTIVE IS LOVE

Now God doesn't discipline us because He enjoys it. He doesn't discipline us in anger. He's never abusive. *Love* is the real reason He disciplines us.

And He loves us so much that He doesn't want us to mess up our lives by sinning. He knows how sin hurts us. So He tries to give us hints and clues along the way. He wants to stop trouble before it ever starts.

THE BIG TURNAROUND

Probably our happiest moments are those that make us say, "Aha!" We suddenly realize what we've done wrong, and we want to make it right. The Bible calls this "repentance."

Bible Snapshot

Stuck in the Wilds

DO YOU REMEMBER how God used Moses to help the Israelites escape slavery in Egypt? God performed all kinds of miracles. He even made countless frogs appear out of nowhere. And then He made the Red Sea split open wide enough so the Israelites could walk through on dry ground.

Now you'd think the Israelites would trust God for anything after that. You'd think they'd want to obey Him. You'd think they'd faithfully follow Moses through the wilderness toward the

Promised Land. But it didn't take long for them to begin to doubt God and disobey.

Even then, God didn't give up on them. When they complained about being hungry, He made food fall from the heavens. When they complained about being thirsty, He made water pour from a rock. He even gave Moses a set of rules, the Ten Commandments, to help them live together more peacefully. Still they doubted God.

Finally, when they reached the border of the Promised Land, the Israelites really blew it. Despite all that God had done for them, and all the instructions and warnings He'd given them, they decided to go their own way. God had promised to give them this beautiful place filled with wonderful things. But no one really believed He would—except for Moses and a couple of other guys. Most of them were simply too scared to cross the border. They didn't trust that God would take care of them over there. And so God told them to go back and wander in the wilderness—for forty more years!

They'd gotten so close to the Promised Land that they could smell the milk and honey. Yet they chose to doubt. Their disobedience forced them back to the desert for the rest of their lives.

We *repent* when we stop our wrong behavior and turn around to face God. Full of regret and shame, we tell God what we've done and ask Him to forgive us.

And He does!

Not only does He forgive us, but He also uses the whole thing to teach us. Hopefully, we'll never make that same mistake again.

God knows we'll make mistakes. He just wants us to get better at obeying.

Does this mean we won't blow it again? Of course not! And God knows we'll make mistakes. He just wants us to get better at obeying. And He wants us to learn to come running back as quickly as possible when we've disobeyed.

Each new day, we need to give God—the vinedresser—our permission to shape, cleanse, support, and redirect us. We need to trust that He really does know what's best for us.

And we can look forward to the future with "grape" expectations. Every vinedresser knows that once a branch starts to grow and thrive, fantastic fruit can't be far behind!

Chapter Five

Shear Madness?

One spring, we moved our family to the country. Our new home had lots of green grass and fresh air. It even had a grapevine growing along the fence!

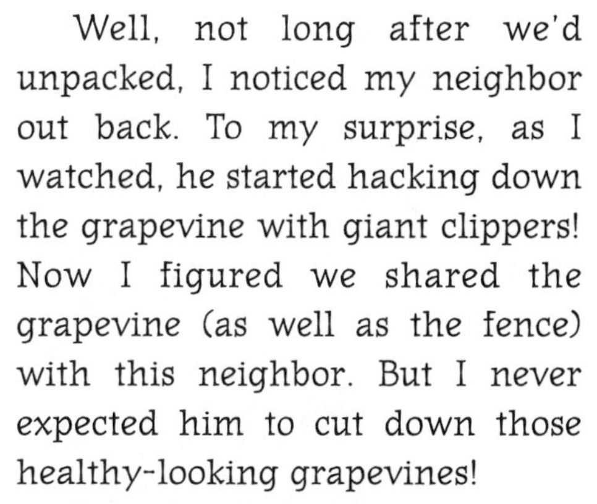

Well, not long after we'd unpacked, I noticed my neighbor out back. To my surprise, as I watched, he started hacking down the grapevine with giant clippers! Now I figured we shared the grapevine (as well as the fence) with this neighbor. But I never expected him to cut down those healthy-looking grapevines!

I tried to hide my concern as I hurried across the backyard. I politely greeted my neighbor, a large white-haired man in overalls. In his hands he held the biggest set of shears I'd ever seen. And all around him lay huge heaps of grapevine cuttings.

"I guess you don't like grapes," I said, trying to act casual.

"Love grapes," he said.

"Really? Well, I thought maybe we would share this grapevine and . . ." I paused, glancing at the green piles around my feet. Maybe I was too late to save this grapevine.

He eyed my shiny shoes. "You're a city boy, aren't ya?" he asked.

"Not exactly, but I . . ."

"Don't know about grapes, do ya?" He went back to his hacking.

I told him I knew I liked the way grapes tasted. And I told him this row of grapes had impressed me when I bought the place.

"You like big, juicy grapes?" he asked over his shoulder.

"Oh yeah. My family does, too," I said.

"Well, son, we can either grow ourselves a lot of beautiful leaves, enough to fill up this whole fence line. Or we can have the biggest, juiciest, sweetest grapes you've ever seen." He looked at me. "We just can't have both."

MORE WITH LESS

We know that God gets involved in our lives when our branches have gotten fruitless and bare because we've sinned. That's when He disciplines us. But what does He do when those branches look pretty good? What if we look like that rambling vine on my fence, but the basket beneath has plenty of room for more grapes?

The vinedresser's secret for creating more is to start with less.

After Jesus told His disciples about the branch without grapes, maybe He picked up one with lots of leaves but only a few grapes. This is what He said next: *"Every branch that bears fruit He prunes, that it may bear more fruit"* (John 15:2).

God's plan is to make a bigger harvest, but His methods might surprise you. To make more, He plans to *prune,* which means to thin, reduce, or cut away. This might sound a bit backward: *The vinedresser's secret for creating more is to start with less.*

My neighbor already understood this when I asked him, "Why are you pruning the vine? Those branches don't look so bad. Have they done something wrong?"

He put down his shears and looked me right in the eyes. His answer surprised me.

"Son," he explained, "these branches have not done anything wrong. But once I cut back the leafy parts, the branches will get stronger. The plant can direct its energy to growing grapes instead of leaves."

Suddenly, what Jesus said in John 15 began to make more sense to me.

Oh! I get it, I thought. The vine sends energy to the branches. But the vinedresser prunes away the unnecessary parts so the vine can send more energy to the growing grapes. Suddenly, what Jesus said in John 15 began to make more sense to me.

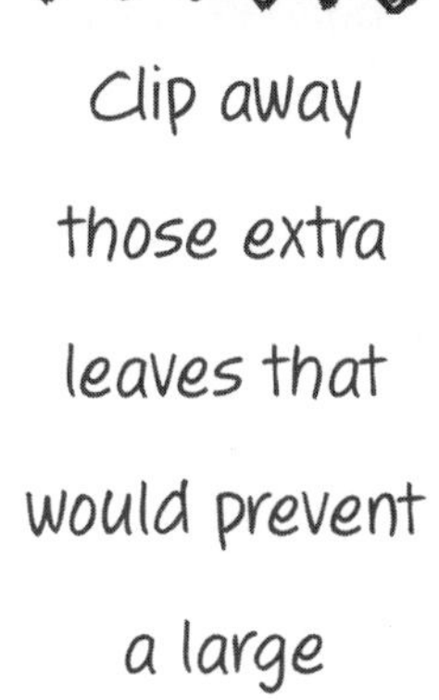

Jesus' disciples had a major advantage over us. They really understood the workings of a vineyard well enough to know that to produce grapes, *you must prune*. Grapevines grow so fast that they can become overloaded with heavy, useless wood. And when that happens, there's no room left for grapes! The whole purpose of a vineyard is to produce grapes. So they knew that a good vinedresser keeps his pruning tools sharpened. That way, he can clip away those extra leaves that would prevent a large harvest. And a good vinedresser knows just the right balance between the leaves and the branches. He knows where to cut and when and why.

But the disciples might not have understood what this pruning business meant to them as Jesus' followers. And maybe you're scratching your head right now, too. *Surely,* you may be thinking, *God doesn't plan to prune off an arm or a leg.* Of course not! But when we really choose to follow God, no matter what, He knows it's time to get out the shears. Maybe He'll prune some of your activities so you'll have more time for His work. Or, maybe He'll prune your group of friends to focus your energy. But whatever He does, you will grow stronger—just like branches on a grapevine.

Whatever He does, you will grow stronger—just like branches on a grapevine.

Now if you can trust God with this—if you believe that He knows what He's doing—then you are ready for the second secret of the vine.

SECOND SECRET OF THE VINE

If your life bears some fruit and God sees that you want to do more for Him, He will prune and redirect your life so that you can do more for Him.

PROFILES IN PRUNING

A good vinedresser prunes in four ways:

1. To remove dead or dying branches,
2. To help sunlight reach the fruit-bearing branches,
3. To increase the size and quality of existing fruit, and,
4. To encourage new fruit to develop.

He wants to remove those things that might hurt us.

Our vinedresser works along the same lines. He wants to remove those things that might hurt us or distract us from serving Him. The following stories show how four kids allowed God to prune in their lives.

Ashur accepted Jesus at summer camp just before he started middle school. But some of his old friends teased him when they found out. They also made fun of him for going to youth group on Wednesday nights. He liked his old friends, but he knew that some of the things they liked to do were wrong. They used bad language, and some of them smoked. Ashur felt frustrated and confused.

Finally, Ashur realized that God wanted him to start hanging out with his new Christian friends. It wasn't easy at first. His old buddies still gave him grief sometimes. But soon Ashur started to feel happier. Then one of his old friends asked if he could go to youth group with Ashur and his new friends.

God showed Ashur that some of his old friends weren't good for him. God pruned Ashur's list of friends so he could grow and become closer to God.

Maria had been a Christian for a while. But she knew she could be selfish—especially with her younger sister, Sofia. Whenever Sofia asked to

She knew it was wrong. Finally, she asked God for help.

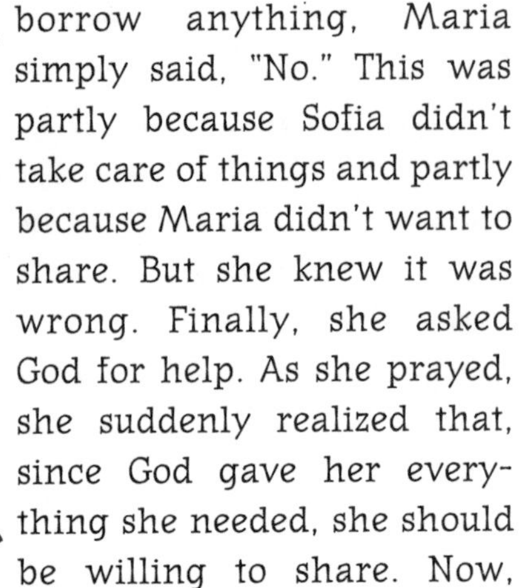

borrow anything, Maria simply said, "No." This was partly because Sofia didn't take care of things and partly because Maria didn't want to share. But she knew it was wrong. Finally, she asked God for help. As she prayed, she suddenly realized that, since God gave her everything she needed, she should be willing to share. Now, whenever her sister asks to borrow something, Maria tries very hard to say, "Yes." And she feels much happier being unselfish.

Sam really wanted to pray and read his Bible, but between swimming and violin practices, tae kwon do, homework, and church activities, he just couldn't find the time. Finally, he asked God to help him make more time. Sam sat down and made a list of all his activities. Then he studied the list. Something had to go. He really liked his tae kwon do classes, but they were held on the other side of town. And his mom never seemed too psyched about driving him there. That night Sam announced that he wanted to quit tae kwon do. Everyone seemed relieved. And now he had more time to spend with God!

On Megan's eleventh birthday, her grandpa gave her fifty dollars. She was so excited that she couldn't wait to spend it. She thought about all the things she could buy. She had almost made up her mind to get a new video game when she saw a news story about children starving in Somalia. She asked her mom if there was some way to help them, and together they found a good organization.

Megan sent a big portion of her birthday gift to feed starving kids. She's also started doing regular chores to earn money to send each month. Megan says doing this makes her happier than a whole pile of new video games!

These kids were all willing to *give up something* once they realized it wasn't helping them to serve God. But they discovered that when they allowed God to prune something away, they ended up with even more. That's how the vinedresser works! He shows us what we need to let go of. These things aren't necessarily bad, but they keep us from having God's best. And then He blesses us with something worth much, much more!

These kids were all willing to *give up something* once they realized it wasn't helping them to serve God.

GIVE IN TO THE SHEARS

God knows what's best for us, but He never forces us to accept it. He always gives us freedom to choose—right or wrong. Even when it comes to pruning, He lets us choose.

God knows what's best for us, but He never forces us to accept it.

First, He shows us what needs to go. Then He waits for us to be willing to let it go. He wants us to trust Him so much that we allow Him to shape us into the kind of branch that will bear lots of fruit. The secret to pruning success is to simply *let go and let God prune you to become the most fruitful branch in His vineyard!*

passed!!!
Pruning Test
Less Leaves & More Fruit.

CHAPTER SIX
"Grape" Expectations!

This chapter will take the idea of being a fruitful branch to a whole new level. Remember, a fruitful branch is a believer who stays close to Jesus, loves others, obeys God, and serves Him by helping others. But wait: There's more.

Some grownups might think I should leave this next section out (since this book is for kids). But I happen to know that kids sometimes understand this part even better than adults do. It all depends on where your relationship with the Lord is. If you really want to give your all for God, then keep reading. If you're still a beginner at walking with the

Lord, you might want to skip this chapter for now. You can always read it later.

"GRAPE" POTENTIAL

As branches mature and bear good fruit, the vine-dresser will prune them even more. Maybe this doesn't make sense to you. Maybe you're thinking, *But if the branch is doing okay and putting out good grapes, why keep pruning it?*

Well, when a branch gets stronger, its potential to make bigger and better fruit increases. But the only way for this to happen is by pruning. The fruit will grow in the following season.

I happen to know **that kids sometimes understand** this part even **better** than **adults** do.

KING-SIZE CHOICES

When we're really serious about loving and serving God, and we tell Him so, He helps us make king-size choices. He wants to be the most important thing in our lives. When we're ready to make king-size choices, we become willing to think about what's most important to us. If it's not God, then we move it to second place in order to put God first in our lives.

God doesn't want us to love anyone more than we love Him.

Sometimes this seems hard, but with God's help, it becomes possible. Here are some of the most common things people have to move to let God be number one:

1. The People You Love the Most

God doesn't want us to love anyone more than we love Him—not even our parents. God wants you to obey your folks, for sure. But He wants you to

This is where faith gets real!

love Him, the Lord, more than anything or anyone. If you know a person that you value more than God, He will ask you to move him or her to second place. But the great thing is, once you put God in first place, you can love others better than ever before. So nobody loses! Love God most, and you can love others better.

2. The Reasons "Why"

For some reason, we think we have the right to know *why* things happen the way they do. And we think we should have control over our lives. But God often does things we'll never understand (at least not here on earth). While we can always ask God for an explanation, He doesn't owe us one.

This is where faith gets real! God wants us to trust Him completely. He wants us to be able to say: "Father, I'm hanging on to You, and You can do whatever You want. Just carry me through."

3. Love of Stuff

We spend our time on what we love. And if we love having lots of cool stuff, we probably spend lots of time with it. But God wants us to have plenty of time to serve Him. So make sure your stuff takes second place to God.

4. Your Own Importance

We all have something that makes us special. You might have a gift in sports or music. Maybe you have lots of friends and activities or you can work through a video game in record time. You might even be serving God in some way in your church or your neighbor-hood. All these things can be good, as long as you keep them in their proper place.

When you allow anything (no matter how good) to become more important than God, it's time to rethink your priorities.

Bible Snapshot

A Boy with King-Size Dreams

EVEN AS A YOUNG BOY, Joseph had amazing dreams about becoming an important man someday. And since he served God, he believed He would eventually make the dreams come true. But Joseph's older brothers were jealous. One day, they sold Joseph as a slave to traveling merchants.

Even living as a slave and far from his homeland, Joseph didn't give up on God or his dreams. And before long, he worked his way into a good

job. Things were really looking up for Joseph, until his boss's wife lied about him and had him thrown into prison. But even in prison, Joseph held tight to God—and his dreams. In prison, God helped Joseph to help others by explaining their dreams to them. Before long, Joseph had a reputation for being unusually wise.

The king of Egypt had some disturbing dreams. He asked Joseph: "What is the meaning of my dreams?"

"God is warning you," Joseph said. "You must store food so your people won't starve when famine strikes."

The king believed Joseph and God. He freed Joseph and hired him to oversee the enormous project of storing seven years' worth of food. You see, Joseph didn't go to prison because he'd done something wrong. He'd done something right. And God continued to prepare him—even in prison—for a greater life.

In time, Joseph's dreams came true. God made him a powerful man in Egypt, and it wasn't long before his older brothers came begging for food. Naturally, Joseph forgave them and shared the food he'd helped to store. This all happened because Joseph believed in God and king-size dreams!

But when you allow anything (no matter how good) to become more important than God, it's time to rethink your priorities.

KING-SIZE HARVEST

Joseph put God and His kingdom first. He trusted God despite some pretty bad circumstances. And in the end, Joseph participated in an amazing harvest. The same thing can happen today with us. When we put God first and trust

Him above all else, we put ourselves in a position to bear lots of fruit. And best of all, we glorify God when we present Him with an incredible king-size harvest!

Chapter Seven

Hang On!

Andre gave his life to Jesus in kindergarten. Even though he was only five, he meant it. By the time he reached middle school, he'd seen God do all sorts of amazing things in his life. But on his thirteenth birthday, Andre felt a little depressed.

"I don't know what's wrong with me," he admitted to Luke, his youth pastor. "I mean, just last month I worked really hard on our fund-raiser for that orphanage in the Ukraine. We raised buckets of cash for those kids. And I go to church and youth group. I study my Bible every day. I've even been memorizing those verses you gave us. I just don't know what else to do."

"Maybe that's the problem," said Luke.

"Huh?" Andre scratched his head. "What do you mean?"

"Maybe you're trying to *do* too much."

"But I thought I was supposed to go all out for God. You always say that we're supposed to—"

"Wait a minute." Luke held up his hands. "Going all out for God is one thing. But is it possible that some of the stuff you're doing is actually going all out for Andre?"

Andre considered this. "You mean like when I do something good and someone comes along and pats me on the back?"

"The problem is we sometimes get so caught up in *doing* good things *for* God that we forget about *being* with God."

"Sort of. Now there's nothing wrong with being appreciated. But the problem is, we sometimes get so caught up in *doing* good things *for* God that we forget about *being with* God."

Cool and unexpected things started to happen at school and at home.

"Being?" Andre frowned. "What do you mean?"

"Being . . ." Luke leaned back and looked up at the ceiling. "Try just *being* God's for a while. Spend some time *being* available to listen to Him. . . . Maybe *being* willing to hang tight with Him and *being* who He wants you to be."

"Being? Not only doing?" Andre asked.

"Yeah, give it a try. You see, when we get caught up in *doing*, it eventually robs us of our joy. But when we learn how to simply *be* God's and *be* who He wants us to be, eventually, we begin to do things for the right reasons."

"I think I get it." Andre thanked Luke and went home to think about this idea some more.

In the days that followed, Andre focused his thoughts on *being* God's. He spent more time just talking to God—and listening, too. And by the end of the week, he felt excited and invigorated. Then cool and unexpected things

started to happen at school and at home. Andre found new opportunities to do things for God. He felt certain that they came from his being in relationship with God.

STAY CONNECTED

That last night in the vineyard, Jesus told His disciples: *"Abide in Me, and I in you. As the branch cannot bear fruit of itself, unless it abides in the vine, neither can you, unless you abide in Me"* (John 15:4).

This could be the most powerful secret of them all. Jesus knew that we could never make it on our own. He knew that if any good fruit would come out of our lives, it would have to come through our relationship with Him. Just like the branch needs to rely on the vine to grow and produce fruit, we need to rely on Jesus. And the good news is that He's relying on us, too!

I know that Jesus wants His meaning to be perfectly clear.

YOUR MAIN ASSIGNMENT

So a branch's number one responsibility is to "abide in the vine." That means to *stay connected to the vine*. To hang on—and hang on tight! Because who knows what might come along next. Perhaps a windstorm, freezing rain, or plant-eating pests . . . anything! But the branch that stays connected to the vine will stay strong and healthy. And best of all, it will have fruit—big, luscious fruit. The more connected the branch stays to the vine, the more the vine's energy will flow through it. And that can mean lots of fruit!

Christians also discover more joy—God's joy, the joy of Christ living inside us! *"These things I have spoken to you, that My joy may remain in you, and that your joy may be full"* (John 15:11).

MORE WITH LESS

But here's what's really cool about abiding. It's not that hard to do. Remember how Andre felt depressed? He thought he had to work so hard and do all kinds of good stuff. But then Luke explained how "being God's" was more important than doing things.

That's what it means to abide, to stay connected. Just make sure that your relationship with Jesus is tight. Make Him your best friend, and try to be His, too!

Bible Snapshot

WHO'S CALLING, PLEASE?

BEFORE KING DAVID'S TIME, a small boy named Samuel went to live at the tabernacle (a place of worship) to serve God. This was quite an honor for a young child. Samuel loved God and took his job very seriously. He wore special clothes and helped the old priest Eli with his duties around the tabernacle.

One night, a voice woke up young Samuel. "Here I am!" he said as he ran to find old Eli. "Did you call me?"

"I didn't call you," said Eli with a sleepy yawn. "Go back to bed."

But again Samuel heard someone calling his name. And again he rushed to Eli's side. "Here I am!" he said eagerly.

"I didn't call you," said Eli again. "Now go back to bed, child."

The third time this happened, Eli realized that God was calling the boy.

"Go to bed, Samuel," said Eli. "And the next time God calls you, *listen*."

Samuel went back to bed. But how could he possibly go back to sleep? Did God really want to speak to him—a young boy?

Once again God called out: "Samuel! Samuel!"

This time Samuel stood at attention and said, "Speak to me, Lord, for I am listening."

God spoke and Samuel listened—and then the boy obeyed. God was pleased with Samuel because, from that day on, Samuel always listened to God and he always obeyed.

In other words, Samuel *abided* with God. They remained great friends, and over the years, God blessed Samuel greatly. God even made him one of the most important leaders in Israel's history.

Go to Him with everything. If you do, you can't help but bear good fruit. How simple is that?

PAY ATTENTION

But how do you know when you're *not* abiding? First of all, you might notice that your inner joy has gone—maybe you feel grumpy or sad or just plain "blah." Then you need to ask yourself: *When was the last time I really talked to God? When was the last time I read His Word and tried to hear what He had to say to me?*

This book is full of new **information** and **challenges.** Take a moment to think about what's most important—hanging tight **with Jesus.** Is He your best friend? Do you tell Him **everything** and involve **Him** in every part of **your life?** Ask Him how you could **tighten** your **relationship** with Him. Then **do it!**

Neglecting any of these things is a sure sign that we're not abiding. And when we quit abiding, we're like a branch that is barely hanging on. We become weak, and our grapes start to look like shriveled raisins.

So, hang in there with God. Hold on to Him like He's holding on to you. The result will be joy and lots of sweet fruit!

FIVE WAYS TO ABIDE

1. Talk to God—not just once a day, but throughout the day. He'll always listen!

2. Read your Bible—set aside a special time each day.

3. Go to church or youth group—regularly!

4. Show God's love to those around you. Even when others don't treat you right, you can show them God's love in action!

5. Do what pleases God—for example, obey your parents, do your homework without making a fuss, and try to make friends with those who feel left out.

CHAPTER EIGHT

The *Best* Friend

Have you already started to do the things on the "abide" list? Why do you think God wants you to do them? Why does He want you to talk to Him and read the Bible? Does He want to make sure you're disciplined? Do you suppose He keeps a checklist up in heaven so His angels can keep track of your habits?

Not even!

The reason God wants you to do these things is that He wants to be your very best friend. He wants you to spend time with Him—talking to Him, reading His message to you (the Bible). He enjoys your company, and He wants you to enjoy His.

So think about it . . . what qualities do you like most in a best friend? Do you want someone who is:

- Always there for you?
- A good listener?
- Accepting of you?
- Trustworthy and loyal?
- Willing to forgive you when you blow it?
- Understanding?
- Ready to love you no matter what?

Well, I've just described the friendship God wants to give each of us. And no one else can be this kind of friend all the time. Admit it, even your best friend can let you down sometimes or get mad at you. Not so with God. He's always there, just waiting for you to say, "Hey, here I am, God. Let's talk."

BEING WITH GOD

Grant rededicated his life to God shortly after he turned twelve. He wanted to serve God in bigger and better ways but wasn't sure how to start. His youth pastor suggested that he start having "quiet times" with God.

Grant decided to do this at night, before bed. But he kept falling asleep, which was pretty frustrating. Since Grant really wanted to know God better, he decided to try setting his alarm clock thirty minutes earlier. Then he could get up and spend time with God before his day started. It took a couple of weeks before Grant could do this regularly. But it didn't take long to see the changes it brought—mostly in himself.

Whenever Grant felt worried or scared or happy, he found himself talking to God.

Grant soon found himself talking to God, not only in the mornings, but off and on throughout the day. Whenever Grant felt worried or scared or happy, he found himself talking to God—just like with a best friend.

Bible Snapshot

God's Good Friend

Remember Moses? He freed Israel from slavery, led the people out of Egypt, and parted the Red Sea for them to cross. Well, did you know that before he became mighty—before he stood up to Pharaoh and God helped him perform miracles—he was just a regular guy? He led a quiet life and tended to his father-in-law's sheep. Not very glamorous. In fact, Moses even had a problem speaking in front of crowds.

So why did God choose Moses to do such incredible things? Why did God make him into one of the greatest heroes of the Bible?

The answer is simple. God called and Moses answered. God had probably had His eye on Moses for a long, long time.

Moses had grown up in Egypt, living a life fit for a king. Then he found out that he was an Israelite (one of the people Egypt had taken as slaves).

After making a major mistake, Moses left for the desert where he led a lonely life. Perhaps this lonely time was his season of pruning and growing—his chance to get close to God. Finally, after many years, God knew it was time to use Moses to do mighty things.

But when Moses realized exactly what God wanted him to do, he got pretty scared. "Who am I?" he asked. "How can I possibly bring the children of Israel out of Egypt?"

And here's the key. God said: *"I will be with you."* It was God's promise that He would stay with Moses the whole time. And like two best friends, Moses and God went off to do the impossible. And the rest is history!

THANK YOU, LORD.

And that's exactly what God became to Grant and Moses—*a real best friend!*

You see, God doesn't just love you, *He also likes you!* He wants to be your best friend, and He wants you to be His!

So, think about it: God's love for us is endless, and Jesus promises to never leave us or forsake us. Wow! Can you make that kind of guarantee back? Being human, it's a bit scary, isn't it? But here's the good news: Even if we fail at being God's best friend, He'll never stop being our best friend. He'll always be right there for us, ready to welcome us back.

How rude!

CHAPTER NINE
Humongous Harvest!

t's not polite to ask for more when someone gives you something. For example, if Grandma gives you a ten-dollar bill for your birthday, you shouldn't say, "Can I have three more of these?" Or if you're eating at your friend's house, you don't ask for seconds on dessert. That would be rude.

Not so with grapes and God. He wants you to really want more—lots more. He knows that means you want more of Him. And you can never get too much of God.

LITTLE MAN, HUGE HARVEST

Deep in the Old Testament is the story of an ordinary guy. He wanted some extraordinary things in his life. And he wasn't afraid to ask for them. Jabez prayed that God would bless him a lot and give him more territory. But that's not all. Jabez also asked God to keep His hand on him and to keep him from evil so he wouldn't hurt anyone. That's a pretty big request.

But God didn't let Jabez down. And although Jabez started out as nothing special (in fact, his name actually means "pain"), the Bible clearly says that God answered his prayer. Instead of living a small, insignificant life, Jabez lived big for God. In other words, he enjoyed a huge harvest!

GIVE YOUR ALL FOR GOD

So, now it's up to you. What do you do with the amazing *Secrets of the Vine*? How do you grow into the kind of branch that will produce a bountiful harvest?

You put God first in your life—you cling to Him with everything you've got. Eventually, the rest will come.

What if you wanted to become a gold-medal

marathon runner? Where would you start? Would you spend your time thinking about what a gold medal looks like? Or imagining how it would feel hanging around your neck? Would you dream about how the crowds would clap and cheer as you crossed the finish line? Not if you wanted to win.

What do you do with the amazing *Secrets of the Vine?*

If you wanted to win, you'd start by lacing up your running shoes and taking off. You'd put one foot in front of the other, and you'd run and run and run. Every day, come rain or snow, you'd get outside and run. In the beginning, you might not even make it around the track. But in time you'd improve. And, maybe, after years of hard work and thousands of miles, you'd get your chance to compete for a medal. Then you'd lace up your running shoes and run that race with everything you've got. But what a prize if you should win!

Bible Snapshot

All to Jesus

MAYBE YOU'VE HEARD about the boy who shared his lunch with Jesus one day. Since we don't know his name, let's call him Ezra. He wanted to go hear Jesus speak. So, being a prepared kind of kid, Ezra took the time to pack himself a nice lunch of bread and fish.

Ezra worked his way through the huge crowd. Finally, he found a spot where he could see and hear Jesus. Then he listened to Jesus speak. And he never got around to eating his lunch.

When suppertime came, Ezra must have been

pretty hungry. Maybe he noticed how many people around him hadn't thought ahead, like he had, to pack a picnic lunch. Maybe he even smiled to himself, thinking about how good his bread and fish would taste.

But then Jesus asked His disciples to see if anyone had any food to share with the hungry crowd. What do you suppose happened to Ezra in that moment? Somehow, Ezra knew he should hand over his lunch. This young man had reached a point of complete trust that day. Ezra handed over his lunch right along with his heart. He knew that both would be safe in Jesus' hands.

That's when Ezra witnessed a miracle: His small lunch of bread and fish was multiplied into enough food for thousands of people! Can you imagine his joy as he stuffed himself with more food than he'd even packed in the first place? Although his bread had been slightly stale, this tasted fresh and delicious. And the fish was unlike any he'd ever tasted before!

You see, Ezra had handed over what little he had that day. But in return he received everything he'd ever need—faith that would carry him through his lifetime and into eternity, faith in the Loving Son of the living God!

Well, no one can guarantee you a gold medal. But if you give your all for God and stay connected to Jesus, you are guaranteed a prize that will never rust or fade or tarnish. You will have a humongous harvest that will make God look down on you and smile, saying, "Well done, My child!"

And nothing on this earth can compare to that.

Your earthly life will be much happier if your goal is to present a humongous harvest to God.

A CHALLENGE

Someday we're all going to stand before God, and one by one we'll lay our harvest at His feet. Whether it's a couple of shriveled raisins or a whole boatload of luscious grapes is entirely up

to you. But I can promise you this: Your earthly life will be much happier if your goal is to present a humongous harvest to God. Because that's what He's designed you for. He made you so that, like a branch, you can cling to the vine. Hang on to Jesus, and prepare to be amazed!

So, how much time do you spend with Jesus each day? Do you think He wants you to spend more? Ask Him how much more. Get specific and write down whatever He places on your heart. Then invite Him to fill your life with fruit as a result. Wait and see what happens next!